Beauty and the Beast

Belle's Story

Adapted from the animated film by
Vanessa Elder

New York

Printed in the United States of America.

First Edition
1 3 5 7 9 10 8 6 4 2

The text for this book is set in 16-point Berkeley Book.

Library of Congress Catalog Card Number: 97-80046

ISBN: 0-7868-4182-6

Contents

CHAPTER ONE
True Beauty

My name is Belle, which means *beautiful* in French.

Sometimes I think beauty was wasted on me. It may sound strange, but the way I look just doesn't seem to matter. Days will go by before I even think to look in a mirror.

I've always loved books. More than anything.

That's not quite true. I love my father more than anything, and I love books more than anything after him.

If not for books—why, I'd be so very bored and lonely in this little town. There's no one here to talk to, no one who shares my interests or feelings. They're all so . . .

Sometimes I wonder—doesn't anyone in this village dream?

"I'll see you later, Papa!" I call as I walk out the door.

It's a beautiful morning. But ever since my father and I came here, my mornings are all the same.

"Good morning, Belle," the baker cheerfully calls as I pass.

"Good morning, monsieur," I reply.

"Where are you off to?" he asks.

"The bookshop," I say. "I just finished the *most* wonderful story about a beanstalk and an ogre and . . ."

"That's nice," he says quickly. He's not interested. He's just being polite.

I know that people in this town don't quite know what to think about me. They think I'm odd. They talk about me behind my back. After all, what pretty girl spends all her free time with her nose in a book?

I happen to like dreaming and thinking.

How else will I figure out life's mysteries? I'm not the kind of person who lets other people tell me how I should be. If they want me to be just like them, well—that's just too bad.

At the same time, I wish I had some friends in this town. One real friend is all I'd want.

The bookshop is my favorite place. Papa and I are poor, but the bookseller is kind to me—he lets me borrow his books as long as I take good care of them. At least *someone* in this town doesn't mind that I love to read!

"Ah, Belle!" he greets me.

"Good morning," I say. "I've come to return the book I borrowed."

"Finished already?"

"Oh, I couldn't put it down," I reply. "Have you got anything new?"

"Not since yesterday!" he chuckles.

"That's all right," I say, scanning the shelves. "I'll borrow . . . this one!"

"That one?" he laughs. "But you've read it twice!"

"Well, it's my favorite! Far off places, daring sword fights, magic spells, a prince in disguise. It's got everything!"

"If you like it that much, it's yours."

"But sir!" I cry.

"I insist."

"Well, thank you," I say. "Thank you very much." How very kind of him!

As I walk home, I stop to sit down on the edge of the fountain and start to read. I love the part where the girl meets Prince Charming—

A manly voice interrupts my dream. "Hello, Belle."

It's not Prince Charming. It's Gaston. My *least* favorite person.

I can't understand why all the girls love him. He's such a brute. Why do I have to be the unlucky one he fancies? All he does is try and get me to pay attention to him, but all he cares about is himself.

"Bonjour, Gaston," I say.

Oh! He snatches the book right out of my hands. He's such a bully!

"Gaston, may I have my book please?" I ask, trying to control my voice.

He holds it out of my reach and flips through the pages.

"How can you read this?" he demands "There are no pictures."

"Well, some people use their imaginations," I explain patiently.

"Belle," he announces, "it's about time you got your head out of those books and paid attention to more important things." He grins smugly. "Like me."

He tosses my book aside and it lands in a mud puddle. The nerve!

I pick my book up out of the puddle. How I wish he would just leave me alone!

"The whole town is talking about it," he continues. "It's not right for a woman to read. Soon she starts getting ideas, and thinking."

That's the whole point! I clean my poor book off with my apron.

Next, he puts his arm around me and snatches the book out of my hands—again.

"Whaddya say you and me take a walk over to the tavern and take a look at my trophies?" he says.

Oh, how *very* exciting.

"Maybe some other time," I reply, sneaking out from under his arm. "I have to get home to help my father. Good-bye."

Suddenly LeFou, Gaston's mean little sidekick, appears.

"That crazy old loon!" LeFou snickers. "He needs all the help he can get!"

Gaston and LeFou burst out laughing.

"Don't talk about my father that way!" I cry, whirling around to face them. "My father is not crazy. He's a genius!"

At that very moment, there's an explosion inside our cottage. Smoke pours out the windows. I run up the hill in panic. What if Papa is hurt?

I hear Gaston and LeFou laughing behind me. They are so cruel. It's just like them to laugh when someone could be hurt, or worse!

I heave open the cellar doors. The smoke is terrible.

I hear Papa coughing. At least he's alive!

He's stuck inside a barrel. He bounces up and down until it breaks.

"Papa!" I cry.

"How on earth did that happen?" he mutters. "Doggone it."

"Are you all right, Papa?"

"I'm about ready to give up on this hunk of junk!" he cries, kicking his invention in despair.

"You always say that," I say affectionately.

"I mean it this time!" he shouts. "I'll never get this boneheaded contraption to work!"

"Yes, you will," I say soothingly. "And you'll win first prize at the fair tomorrow."

"*Hmph!*"

"And become a world-famous inventor."

"You really believe that?" Papa asks, a twinkle in his eye.

"I always have," I reply.

"Well, what are we waiting for? I'll have this thing fixed in no time. Hand me that dog-legged clincher there."

That's my father! Full of spirit. He's not a man who gives up easily.

"So, did you have a good time in town today?" he asks.

Hardly.

"I got a new book," I say as I hand him a tool.

"Papa," I begin carefully, "do you think I'm odd?"

"My daughter?" he demands. "Odd? Where would you get an idea like that?"

"Oh, I don't know," I sigh. "It's just that I'm not sure I fit in here. There's no one I can really talk to."

"What about that Gaston?" Papa asks. "He's a handsome fellow."

Papa is a genius, but sometimes he can't see the most obvious things.

"He's handsome all right," I say, "and rude and conceited and . . . Oh, Papa, he's not for me."

"Well, don't you worry," Papa says, "because this invention's going to be the start of a new life for us."

He makes some final adjustments. "I think that's done it," he says. "Now, let's give it a try."

Here goes. Papa pulls down a lever and the contraption springs noisily to life, chopping and stacking firewood.

"It works!" I cry.

"It does?" Papa asks, flabbergasted. "Well, so it does!"

"You did it!" I cheer. "You really did it!"

"Hitch up Philippe, my girl!" my father shouts. "I'm off to the fair!"

"Good-bye, Papa! Good luck!" I wave.

"Good-bye, Belle! And take care while I'm gone!"

I'm so proud of Papa. He tries so hard.

CHAPTER TWO

Marry Gaston? Never!

Just as I've finished my chores and settled down in my favorite reading chair, there's a knock at the door. Who could it be? I peer through the peephole.

It's Gaston.

As soon as I unlock the door he pushes past me into the room.

"Gaston. What a pleasant surprise," I say, trying to keep my voice steady.

"Isn't it, though?" he trumpets. "I'm just full of surprises."

"You know, Belle," he continues, "there's not a girl in town who wouldn't love to be

11

in your shoes. This is the day . . ."

He's distracted by the sight of himself in the mirror. I've never met anyone so ridiculously vain! And so inconsiderate!

"This is the day your dreams come true," he finishes.

"What do *you* know about my dreams, Gaston?" I ask annoyed.

"Plenty!" he blusters. "Here. Picture this."

He sits down in my chair and plops his huge muddy feet right on my book. Can't he

figure anything out? My most prized possession and he gets mud all over it! Twice!

He continues fantasizing. "A rustic hunting lodge, my latest kill roasting on the fire . . ."

He kicks off his boots. His feet smell like old cheese.

". . . My little wife massaging my feet, while our little ones play on the floor with the dogs. We'll have six or seven."

"Dogs?" I put in hopefully.

"No, Belle!" he bellows. "Strapping boys—like me!"

"Imagine that!" I sigh. A whole houseful of horrible boys like him.

"And you know who that little wife will be?" he asks.

"Let me think . . . ," I say.

"You, Belle!" he cries.

"Gaston, I'm speechless. I really don't know what to say."

"Say you'll marry me."

"I'm very sorry, Gaston, but . . . I just don't deserve you."

He puckers up to kiss me and closes his eyes. I manage to find the doorknob and open the door just in time. Gaston goes flying out the door, and I slam it shut.

I open the door again, throwing Gaston's smelly boots out after him. I bolt the door tight.

Whew! That was close.

A while later, I peek out.

"Is he gone?" I ask the chickens.

"Can you imagine? He asked me to marry him. Me! The wife of that boorish, brainless . . ."

Now I'm really angry. Who does he think he is? I'll never be his little wife! There's much more to life than that.

I run out to the field and look over the pond. The afternoon sun shines on it so brilliantly. I feel like the whole world is open before me. I settle down on the grass and imagine who my beloved will be. He'll be a man who understands my dreams, who wants to share them. I pick a dandelion and make a wish.

What wonderful things are there for me in this world? I know that adventure must be out there somewhere, because I believe in the stories I read. Even if they are just fairy tales, they seem so real.

CHAPTER THREE
Nightmare

My daydream vanishes in a cold rush as Philippe comes charging through the field.

"Philippe! What are you doing here?" I cry. "Where's Papa? What happened?"

There is a terrified look in the horse's eyes. How I wish he could talk!

"Oh, we have to find him! You have to take me to him!"

I unhitch Philippe from the wagon and we ride deep into the forest. Soon night falls.

Philippe takes me down a strange path. Suddenly an enormous castle looms before me.

"What is this place?" I whisper. It is awesome, dark, forbidding.

I spy Papa's hat on the ground.

Although the castle is the most frightening place I've ever seen, I must go inside.

The heavy door creaks open. "Hello?" I call nervously. "Is anyone here?"

"Hello Papa? Are you here?" I call out.

I see the glow of a candle disappearing up the steps. There *must* be someone here!

"Wait!" I cry. "I'm looking for my father!"

I run up the stairs after the light, but there is no one.

"That's funny," I whisper to myself, "I'm sure there was someone. Is anyone here?"

Suddenly I hear Papa's raspy voice calling me weakly. "Belle?"

And there he is, locked in a prison cell!

"Papa!" I cry.

I run to him and grab his hand through the bars of the cell. He is huddled on the cold stone floor, shivering and coughing.

"How did you find me?" he stammers.

"Oh," I cry. "Your hands are like ice!

17

We have to get you out of here."

"Belle," my father whispers. "I want you to leave this place."

"Who's done this to you?" I demand.

"No time to explain!" he cries, his voice rising. "You must go! Now!"

"No! I won't leave you!"

Suddenly I feel a strong hand grasp my shoulder and tear me away from Papa.

"What are you doing here?" someone yells.

I gasp. I lose my grip on the torch. It flies

out of my hand and goes out. We are now in total darkness.

"Run, Belle!" my father cries.

"Who's there?" I shout. "Who are you?"

I hear the voice come out of the darkness again.

"The master of this castle," it growls.

"I've come for my father," I say. "Please let him out. Can't you see? He's sick."

"Then he shouldn't have trespassed here!"

"But he could die!" I cry. "Please, I'll do anything."

"There's nothing you can do," the master says, his voice filled with disgust. "He's my prisoner."

"Oh, there must be some way I could . . . Wait!" I cry.

I have an idea. I will offer to stay in Papa's place.

"Take me instead," I plead.

"You!" he spits, his voice bitter. Then he pauses, as if amazed that I would do such a thing. "You would take his place?"

"Belle, no!" my father cries frantically.

But I must. I am young and strong, and Papa is old and sick. And I love him. I would do anything for him.

"You don't know what you're doing!"

"If I did," I demand, "would you let him go?"

"Yes," the voice replies.

I press myself against the cold stone wall as I feel the master of the castle lean toward me. I can feel his hot breath, his huge presence. Is he a man or a beast?

"But you must promise to stay here forever," it continues.

Forever!

"Come into the light," I say. I must see him.

I gasp as he steps into the light. He is truly not a man, but a beast unlike any I've ever seen! Even in all of the tales I have ever read!

He is enormous, almost twice the size of a big man, with long, matted brown fur and the

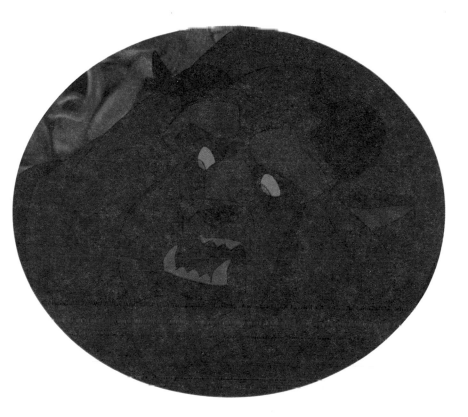

horns of a bull. And his teeth are like a tiger's, and his paws resemble the claws of a lion.

"No, Belle!" my father cries. "I won't let you do this!"

"You have my word," I say to the Beast, summoning all my strength. For my father's sake I will endure anything.

"Done!" the creature says, satisfied.

21

He opens my father's cell.

I sink to my knees.

What have I done? Will I truly be this creature's prisoner forever? And what will he do to me?

My father puts his arms around me desperately.

"No, Belle, listen to me. I'm old. I've lived my life."

The creature grabs my father and drags him mercilessly away.

"Wait!" I cry.

But it is too late. I hear the huge castle doors slam shut with a boom. Through the tower window I can see a spiderlike carriage whisking my father away.

I'll never see Papa again! I'll be locked in this tower forever, like Rapunzel! Only there will be no prince to rescue me!

I begin to cry. I can't fight the despair that engulfs my heart. I'll never be happy again, I'll never even see the light of day again.

CHAPTER FOUR
Enchantment

Once again I feel the shadow of the hateful creature looming over me.

"You didn't even let me say good-bye," I sob. "I'll never see him again. And I didn't get to say good-bye."

"I'll show you to your room," the Beast says.

"My room?" I look up. "But I thought—"

"Follow me," he says gruffly.

"I hope you like it here," the creature says, turning to me. "The castle is your home now, so you can go anywhere you like." Then he quickly adds, "Except the West Wing."

"Wh-what's in the West—," I stammer.

The creature whirls around to face

me, his eyes ablaze.

"It is forbidden!" he thunders. I shrink from his sudden wrath.

"Now," he continues more calmly, "if you need anything, my servants will attend you."

He opens the doors to my room. I step inside and look around nervously. To my surprise, it isn't black or gloomy. It's quite cheerful.

"You will join me for dinner!" he shouts.

With that, he slams the door in my face.

I run across the room and throw myself on the big, soft bed. This is a warmer, prettier prison than the tower, but a prison all the same.

I hear a knock at the door.

"Who is it?" I ask through my tears.

"Mrs. Potts, dear," a motherly voice replies.

I stumble to the door and open it, but there's no one there! Is this a trick?

"I thought you might like a spot of tea." There's a voice coming from the floor.

I can't believe my eyes! A talking teapot bounces into the room.

24

"But you . . . you're a . . . ," I stammer.

In my shock, I back up right into the wardrobe. It springs to life.

"Careful," it laughs, its voice jolly.

"This is impossible!" I cry.

"I told you she was pretty, Mama. Didn't I?" a little teacup chirps.

"All right, Chip. Now, that'll do," his mother says, pouring hot tea into him.

"Slowly now," she warns him, as he hops toward me. "Don't spill."

I kneel down on the floor and pick him up. I've never felt anything so strange as picking up a teacup that's alive!

"Thank you," I manage to say, and sip the tea. It's delicious, and I feel my strength coming back to me.

25

"Wanna see me do a trick?" Chip suddenly asks.

He blows bubbles in my tea.

"Chip!" his mother scolds.

"Oops," he says sheepishly. "Sorry."

"That was a very brave thing you did, my dear," Mrs. Potts says to me.

"We all think so," the wardrobe chimes in.

"But I've lost my father, my dreams, everything," I say. My voice sounds pitiful in my own ears. I'm starting to think that what I did was more foolish than brave.

"Cheer up, child," Mrs. Potts says. "It'll turn out all right in the end. You'll see."

But how can it ever turn out all right?

"Hoo! Listen to me," she continues. "Jabbering on while there's a supper to get on the table." She hops toward the door.

"Chip," she calls. He hops out of my hand and goes to her.

"Bye!" he says.

The doors close behind them.

"Well, now," the wardrobe begins. "What shall we dress you in for dinner?"

She takes out one of the dresses hanging on her rack.

"Ah, here we are! You'll look ravishing in this one."

I shake my head and push the dress away.

"That's very kind of you," I explain, "but I'm not going to dinner."

The wardrobe gasps in fear. "But you must!"

Suddenly a little walking, talking clock darts in, clearing its throat.

"Dinner is served," he announces.

I refuse again. How can they expect me to be sociable knowing I'll never see Papa again?

Suddenly there is the most horrendous pounding on my chamber door.

"I thought I told you to come down to dinner!" It's my captor, and he is furious.

"I'm not hungry," I cry.

"You can't stay in there forever," he bellows.

"Yes, I can!" I retort.

"Fine! Then go ahead. . . . Starve!" he roars, the sound echoing off the stone walls and making my ears ring.

"If she doesn't eat with me, then she doesn't eat at all," he commands, and storms off.

"The master's really not so bad once you get to know him," the wardrobe says softly. "Why don't you give him a chance?"

I start to cry again. "I don't want to get to know him. I don't want to have anything to do with him."

Why should I? He's nothing but a monster.

CHAPTER FIVE
Dinner Is Served

My stomach is growling painfully. It's been hours since my last meal. I wonder if I can find the kitchen. . . .

I step out of my room cautiously and make my way down the grand staircase.

"Splendid to see you out and about, mademoiselle," the little clock says, startled, as I enter the kitchen. "I am Cogsworth, head of the household."

Suddenly a candlestick comes hopping up to us and grabs my hand.

"This is Lumiere," Cogsworth says.

"*Enchanté, cherie*," Lumiere says, and kisses my hand again and again.

"If there's anything we can do to make your stay more comfortable . . . ," Cogsworth begins graciously.

"I *am* a little hungry," I say shyly.

"You are?" Mrs. Potts asks eagerly. "Hear that? She's hungry."

"Stoke the fire," she cries. "Break out the silver. Wake the china."

"Remember what the master said," Cogsworth whispers nervously.

"Oh, pish tosh!" Mrs. Potts says briskly. "I'm not about to let the poor child go hungry."

"All right, fine," Cogsworth says primly. "Glass of water, crust of bread—"

Lumiere interrupts him. "Cogsworth! I

am surprised at you. She's not a prisoner. She's our guest!"

"Well," Cogsworth sputters, "keep it down! If the master finds out about this—"

"Of course, of course," Lumiere says, shrugging off the warning. "But what is dinner without a little music?"

The next thing I know, Lumiere is standing in the center of the dining room table.

"*Ma chère mademoiselle*," he announces, "it is with deepest pride and greatest pleasure that we welcome you tonight. And now, we invite you to relax." A comfortable chair comes rushing up to me. "Let us pull up a chair as the dining room proudly presents—your dinner."

I stare in amazement as the platters take their positions.

There is no way to describe the spectacle that appears before me. I've never seen anything like it! It's clear that I'm the first guest they've had in a small eternity.

I've never had such a marvelous dinner. And I've never been treated so royally in my life. Like a princess in a fairy tale.

I don't understand how such a selfish, unkind master could have such devoted servants.

One thing's certain—this castle is truly enchanted. It's just like something I once read in a book. . . . And yet it's real!

"My goodness, look at the time," Cogsworth says. "Now it's off to bed."

But I'm wide awake! "Oh, I couldn't possibly go to bed now. It's my first time in an enchanted castle, and I'd like to look around if that's all right."

"Oh!" Lumiere exclaims. "Would you like a tour?"

"Eh, wait a second, wait a second," Cogsworth butts in. "I'm not sure that's such a good idea. We can't let her go poking around in *certain places*, if you know what I mean."

"Perhaps you'd like to take me," I say to Cogsworth. "I'm sure you know everything there is to know about the castle."

"Oh, well . . . actually, yes, I do," he says, flattered.

He takes me through the corridors, explaining all the architectural details. He gets very involved in his descriptions, and I take the opportunity to wander off.

Suddenly my path is blocked by a barking footstool, Lumiere, and Cogsworth.

"What's up there?" I ask, pointing up a flight of stairs.

"Where? There?" Cogsworth stammers. "Oh, nothing. Absolutely nothing of interest at all in the West Wing. Dusty, dull, very boring."

"Ah, so *that's* the West Wing," I say, trying to get past them.

Cogsworth tries to dissuade me. "Perhaps mademoiselle would like to see something else. We have exquisite tapestries dating all the way back to . . ."

"Maybe later," I interrupt. I've got to get to the bottom of this mystery!

"Uh," Lumiere adds, "maybe you would like to see the gardens, or the library perhaps?"

I stop in my tracks. "You have a library?"

Cogsworth is overwhelmed with relief. "Oh! Yes. Oh, indeed!"

"With books!" Lumiere exclaims. "Scads of books!"

"More books than you'll ever be able to read in a lifetime."

They march off down the hall, still talking, and I let them think I'm following. I'd love to see the library, of course, but now may be my only chance to get into the West Wing.

At the top of the stairs I see my reflection multiplied a thousand times in a broken mirror. I open a door with knobs that are shaped like monsters' heads.

I gasp at the wreckage before me. This was once such a beautiful room, and now it's . . . ruined. It looks as if the Beast has vented his rage upon the place.

I feel that someone is watching me and I gasp in fright.

But there is no one, only a torn portrait on the wall. The eyes look so real! I can't make out the face.

Suddenly I see a shimmering pink glow in the corner of my eye.

I don't know that I've ever encountered anything so strange—and so beautiful.

It's a rose, a single red rose, under a glass cover, suspended in midair by some enchantment. I wonder what it means? I carefully lift the cover.

Suddenly I hear a loud snarl. My heart leaps to my throat, and I can't breathe.

"Why did you come here?" he demands.

He snatches the glass cover from my hands and slams it protectively over the rose.

"I warned you never to come here!" he shouts.

"I didn't mean any harm!" I explain.

He yells at me with all his might. "Do you realize what you could have done? GET OUT!" he roars. The sound is deafening.

Somehow I get past him. I never want to stop running.

CHAPTER SIX
Wolves

I fly down the stairs. I open the castle door and am met by a gust of wind and snow. I don't care if I freeze out there. If I stay here, the Beast will kill me.

I leap on Philippe's back and we charge through the castle gate.

We've barely ridden a mile when suddenly Philippe whinnies with fear.

We are surrounded by hungry, yellow eyes. Wolves.

I wonder which fate is worse: to be torn apart by a pack of wolves or by the Beast?

We take off at a gallop. We cross a frozen pond, but the ice breaks under Philippe's weight. Bitterly cold water numbs my skin.

Philippe struggles to swim and manages to climb onto solid ground. But the wolves still follow.

Philippe rears back and I am thrown from the saddle. I grab a strong stick and try to fight the wolves off. They snap at my cloak and try to pull me to the ground.

Suddenly something grabs hold of the wolf that is about to leap on my throat.

It is the Beast.

The wolves attack him all at once, but he

fights them with superhuman fierceness and strength.

He hurls the leader off of me and the rest of the pack runs off, crying, into the woods.

All is quiet. The Beast groans and faints.

He must have followed me, knowing the danger I'd meet.

I know that I'm free to ride back home. But the Beast is hurt, and I can't leave him here. Not after he saved my life.

I cover him with my cloak and rouse him. When he comes to, he manages to climb on Philippe's back. I lead Philippe slowly back to the castle.

The Beast's servants are waiting fearfully by the door. They take their exhausted master into his sitting room, where a fire is blazing. Mrs. Potts prepares a basin of hot water.

I nurse his wounds, and he growls in pain. "That hurts!"

"If you'd hold still, it wouldn't hurt as much!" I cry.

"Well, if you hadn't run away, this wouldn't have happened!" he snarls.

"If you hadn't frightened me, I wouldn't have run away!"

"Well, you shouldn't have been in the West Wing!" he scolds.

"Well, you should learn to control your temper!" I snap.

The Beast is vexed, but he can't say anything more. I'm right, after all.

"By the way," I say, "thank you for saving my life."

"You're welcome," he says softly.

His voice can be so surprising. When he roars, I feel as if my eardrums will burst, but when his voice is soft, it is so gentle.

CHAPTER SEVEN
Friends

Something has changed. Since our experience with the wolves, the Beast and I trust each other. We've even come to—like each other. It's so puzzling.

My thoughts are never far from my father, but life in the castle is so pleasant, such a wonderful change from the village.

"Belle," the Beast says, "there's something I want to show you."

He cracks open a door and peeks inside. I try to peer over his shoulder.

"But first," he says, "you have to close your eyes."

I close my eyes to humor him.

41

He takes my hands and leads me through a passageway.

"Can I open them?" I ask.

"No, not yet," he replies. "Wait here."

I hear the sound of a curtain being yanked back and feel sunlight on my face. This room smells familiar. It smells like . . . books!

"Now can I open them?" I ask eagerly.

"All right," he says gently. "Now."

I gasp in awe. "I can't believe it. I've never seen so many books in all my life!"

"It's yours," he says graciously, his blue eyes shining with joy at my pleasure.

I reach out, and my hands hold his paws. "Oh, thank you so much!"

This is the most astounding gift I've ever been given. There *are* more books in this library than I could read in a lifetime.

It's so strange the way the Beast has been changing. He's trying so hard to control his temper and to see past his limitations. Now, instead of roaring about them, he just tries a little harder. And he seems . . . so much happier.

I wonder why I didn't see it there before. His kindness.

Tonight we're having a special dinner. I dress in a beautiful golden gown. And the Beast looks . . . well, handsome!

As we eat our soup, the coatrack begins to play the violin. I can't resist the beautiful music. I grab the Beast's paws and lead him to the magnificent ballroom.

I show him how to waltz, and he picks it

up very quickly. I believe he knew how to dance already. He just had to be reminded.

We step out onto the balcony to rest. It's such a magical night. All the stars are out, and the sky is a deep, dark blue.

"Belle," he says, taking my hands in his paws, "are you happy here with me?"

"Yes," I say. But my face falls. My worries about my father come rushing back to me. I feel guilty about having such a wonderful time when he . . . Why, he must think I'm being tortured every day! Locked in a dank cell! Starving!

"What is it?" the Beast asks, his voice filled with concern.

"If only I could see my father again," I explain. "Just for a moment. I miss him so much."

"There is a way," the Beast says, after thinking for a moment.

He leads me to the forbidden West Wing, to the small table where the poor rose droops under its cover.

He holds up a mirror.

"This mirror will show you anything," he says. "Anything you want to see."

I take it, not sure what to do. "I'd like to see my father, please," I ask politely.

To my astonishment, the mirror glows and shimmers, and my reflection disappears. Suddenly I can see my father struggling against a strong wind in the woods. He collapses before my eyes!

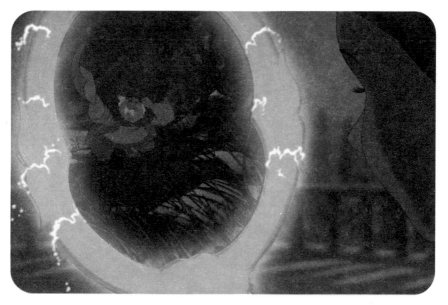

"Papa!" I cry. "Oh no! He's sick. He may be dying, and he's all alone."

"Then you must go to him," my friend says, his voice full of pain.

"What did you say?" I gasp.

"I release you," he whispers, his voice heavy with feeling. "You are no longer my prisoner."

"Oh, thank you," I cry.

I hold the mirror out to my friend, but he refuses to take it.

"Take it with you," he says, "so you'll always have a way to look back and remember me." He strokes my hair with his paw and a shiver runs through me. I don't want to leave, but I must go to my father.

"Thank you," I say, "for understanding how much he needs me."

I stroke the Beast's face and gaze into his beautiful blue eyes.

As Philippe and I ride off, the Beast's anguished howl echoes in the woods all around us.

46

CHAPTER EIGHT
The Mob

Not far from the castle, I find my father lying in the snow.

"Papa!" I cry. He's alive, but he's barely conscious. I help him onto Philippe's back and lead him home.

"Belle!" Papa cries.

"Shh," I say. "It's all right, Papa. I'm home."

"But the Beast," he says fearfully. "Did you—how did you escape?"

"I didn't escape, Papa. He let me go."

It makes my heart break to see how worried Papa has been.

Suddenly Chip hops out of Philippe's saddle bag.

"Belle," he demands, "why did you go away? Don't you like us anymore?"

"Oh, Chip," I say, "of course I do. It's just that—"

My words are cut short by a pounding on the door.

There's a mob of villagers holding torches, led by LeFou!

"May I help you?" I ask uncertainly.

"I've come to collect your father," the man announces.

I look at the man's wagon and see that he's come from the asylum!

"My father is not crazy!" I cry.

"He was raving like a lunatic," LeFou says. "We all heard him, didn't we?"

The townsfolk murmur in agreement. They all want my father locked up!

"No! I won't let you!" I scream.

"Belle?" Papa cries, still groggy.

"Tell us again, old man, just how big was the Beast?" LeFou cackles.

"It's true, I tell you!" my father cries.

"Get him outta here!" LeFou screeches.

"No!" I gasp. "You can't do this!"

Suddenly Gaston appears.

"Poor Belle," he says, his voice dripping with false sympathy. "It's a shame about your father."

"You know he's not crazy, Gaston," I plead.

"*Hmm,*" he says. "I might be able to clear up this little misunderstanding if . . ."

"If what?" I ask.

"If you marry me," he replies.

"What?" I gasp. My blood runs cold.

"One little word, Belle," he says. "That's all it takes."

"Never!" I cry.

"Have it your way," he snarls.

"My father's not crazy," I shout, holding up the magic mirror. "And I can prove it."

"Show me the Beast!" I command.

Everyone cries out in amazement as the mirror reveals my friend roaring in misery.

"Is he dangerous?" a woman asks.

"Oh, no," I say. "He'd never hurt anyone. Please, I know he looks vicious, but he's really kind and gentle. He's my friend."

Gaston grabs me and whirls me round to face him.

"If I didn't know better," he sneers, "I'd think you had *feelings* for this monster."

50

I pull free of his repulsive grasp. "He's no monster, Gaston. *You* are!"

"She's as crazy as the old man!" he yells. "The Beast will make off with your children. He'll come after them in the night!"

"No!" I scream, but it's no use.

"We're not safe till his head is mounted on my wall!" Gaston shouts. "I say we kill the Beast!"

Shouts of "Kill him!" fill the air. I try to wrest the mirror from Gaston's grasp. But it's no use.

"No, I won't let you do this!" I wail.

"If you're not with us," Gaston declares, "you're against us!"

Gaston hurls my father and me into the cellar and bolts the doors.

I try to pry open a window. "I have to warn the Beast," I cry. "This is all my fault."

"Now, now," my father tries to console me. "We'll think of something."

Suddenly there is a noise like a train barreling toward the cellar. A whistle blows.

"Belle, look out!" my father cries.

We leap away just in time as a flying ax blade chops the cellar doors to pieces.

It's Chip, driving my father's wood-chopper. What a clever teacup!

CHAPTER NINE
The Spell Is Broken

We fly to the castle, Philippe galloping at top speed. I must get there before it is too late.

I spy the Beast crouching on the roof. Gaston is looming over him, about to deal him a deathly blow.

"No!" I scream. My voice rings out in the night.

The Beast looks down and sees me there, and I am filled with love.

"No! Gaston, don't!" I cry.

Suddenly, the Beast regains his incredible strength and fights back. Gaston may be stronger than most men, but the Beast is stronger than ten men together.

Philippe and I burst through the castle doors. I run up the stairs and out to the balcony.

"Beast!" I cry.

That's the only time I've ever actually called him that. He looks up at me and smiles.

"Belle," he says, his voice filled with love and tenderness.

I reach my hand down over the railing.

He begins to climb toward me.

"Belle," he says. "You came back."

I smile and touch his paw.

Suddenly he stiffens and roars in pain. Gaston appears behind him, holding a gleaming, bloody dagger. The Beast almost falls, but I grab onto him. Gaston loses his balance and plunges to his death, howling.

The Beast has a great wound in his side. I lay him down on the balcony and gently rest his head on the floor.

He gasps for air. "You came back," he says.

"Of course I came back," I whisper. "I couldn't let them—"

But have they killed him? I throw my arms around my friend and lay my head on his chest.

"Oh, this is all my fault," I sob. "If only I'd gotten here sooner."

"Maybe it's better this way," the Beast gasps and coughs.

"Don't talk like that," I cry. "You'll be all right. We're together now. Everything's going to be fine, you'll see."

He touches my face. "At least," he stammers, "I got to see you one last time."

His head falls back. From the chill that grips my heart I know that he is dead.

"No! No!" I sob. "Please, don't leave me! I love you."

I sob on his silent chest as thunder rumbles and rain begins to fall.

Then I feel something tingling. It's not

rain. I lift my head and see shafts of light falling all around us. I feel the Beast's body stirring beneath me, rising like a feather into the air. His cloak swirls about him, and before my very eyes he turns into a beautiful man.

"Belle," he whispers. "It's me."

His voice is the same. I reach out and touch his hair and look uncertainly into his blue eyes.

"It *is* you," I say.

We kiss, and I am filled with love and amazement. The flame that stirred the life in his breast has entered my heart, too.

"Lumiere! Cogsworth! Oh, Mrs. Potts! Look at us!" the Beast cries, as he hugs his servants. They're all human again! The spell has been broken.

My prince and I waltz around the ball-room.

I hope this night never ends.

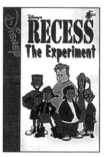

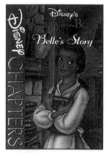

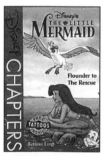

A New World of Adventure Opens at Walt Disney World

Visit Disney's newest theme park, Disney's Animal Kingdom, for an adventure like no other. Go on a heart-pounding expedition into the world of animals on The Kilimanjaro Safari. And in Dinoland, USA, go back 65 million years and witness the end of the dinosaur era—get right in on the action at the thrilling new attraction, Countdown to Extinction. It's all new and it's all amazing.

You can experience the excitement up close with these Disney Press books:

**COUNTDOWN TO EXTINCTION HOLOGRAM BOOK
A HOLOGRAPHIC ADVENTURE
TO PREHISTORIC TIMES**
ISBN 0-7868-3175-8
$16.95 ($22.95 CAN)

**Ðⁱꜱɴᴇᴩ CHAPTERS:
Ðⁱꜱɴᴇᴩ's ANIMAL KINGDOM
COUNTDOWN TO EXTINCTION**
ISBN 0-7868-4235-0
$3.95 ($5.50 CAN)

Available at your local bookstore.

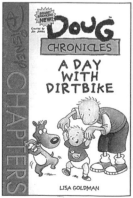